Nanny Paws

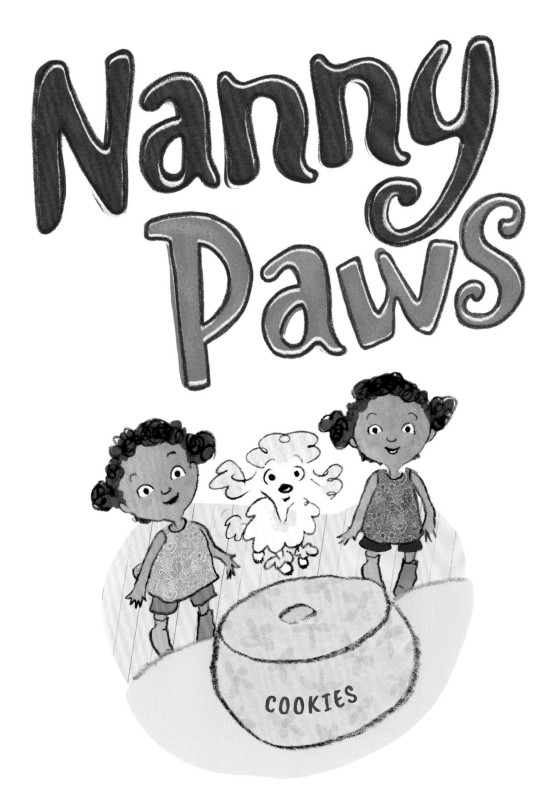

COOKIES

Wendy Wahman

two lions

To Ian and Tierney and their Nanny LaRoo,
and to Devon and her Nanny Duke.

Published by Two Lions, New York
www.apub.com
Amazon, the Amazon logo, and Two Lions are trademarks
of Amazon.com, Inc., or its affiliates.

ISBN-13: 9781503954366 (hardcover)
ISBN-10: 1503954366 (hardcover)

The illustrations are rendered in pencil, watercolor, and digital.
Book design by Abby Dening
Printed in China
First Edition
10 9 8 7 6 5 4 3 2 1

Nanny Paws looks after Ally and Mae.
There's nothing she wouldn't do for her girls.

Why, just last Tuesday
she woke the twins,

washed their faces,

and helped them get dressed.

Chomp, Slurp, Crunch!

cleared the table,

then bagged their lunches.

Good morning, Nanny Paws!

Then Nanny Paws walked Ally and Mae to school and caught up with the other nannies.

Back home,
she picked up toys,

Dig,
Dig,
Dig,
Dig,
Dig!

did a little gardening,

and kept busy until the twins returned.

Good job, Nanny Paws!

But that Tuesday she didn't have long to wait.
Ally and Mae had tummy aches.
They needed their Nanny Paws right away.

Now what had her girls gotten into without her?

Nanny Paws could only imagine.

No matter! Nanny Paws knew just what to do.

First, she made sure their tummies were nice and warm.

Next, she fetched the doctor.

Good job,
Nanny Paws!

She then prescribed bed rest
and sang a lilting lullaby.

When Ally and Mae woke up, they felt much better . . . and a little hungry!

Nanny Paws recommended

chicken soup,

saltines, and . . .

a belly rub.

Good job,
Nanny Paws!

With Ally and Mae nursed back to health, Nanny Paws let them out for some fresh air and exercise.

First, a little yoga (with plenty of downward dogs),

then a game of catch.

Whooosh!

After a long day, they settled in for the night with a calming bedtime story.

Woof, woof!

Yap, yap, woof!

Bark!

BARK, BARK!

Yip Yip!

Yip. Yip!

WOOF!

Yippy yap!

Lick, Lick, Lick!

When it was time for their bath, Nanny Paws tested the water,

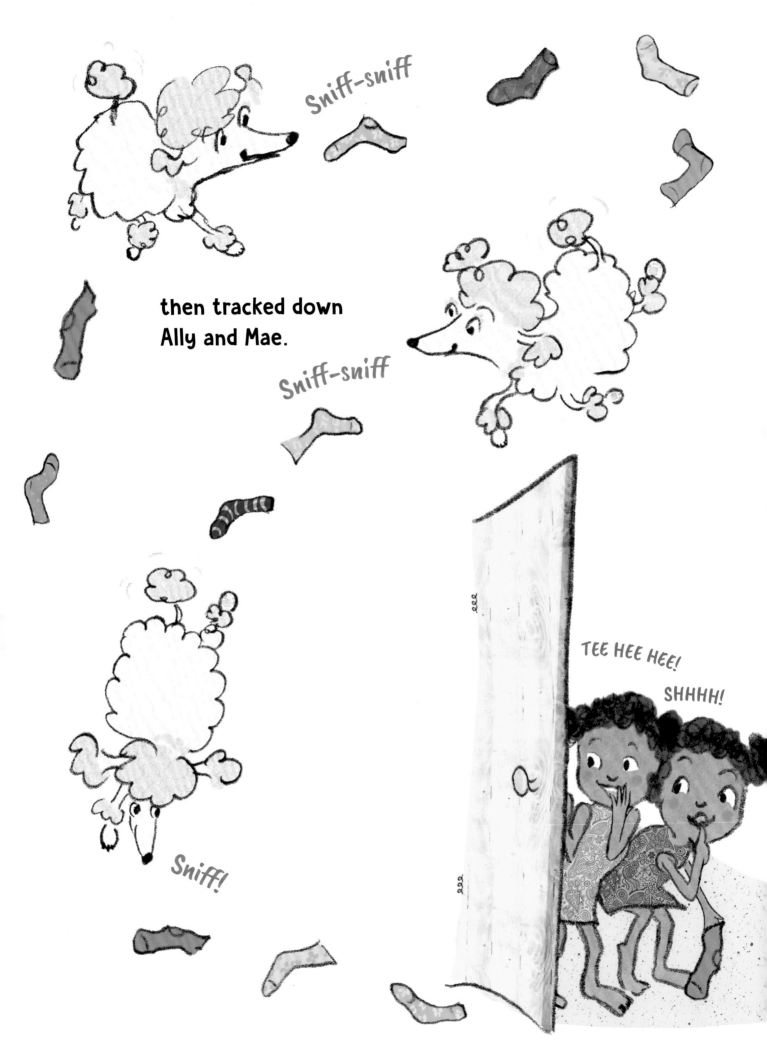

then tracked down
Ally and Mae.

Who knew being a nanny was such hard work?

But she wouldn't trade a minute of it.

Not that Tuesday, or any other day.

Good night, Nanny Paws.
Sleep tight!